CLAUDIA & Moth

BY

Jennifer Hansen Rolli

VIKING

Claudia loved butterflies.

In the summertime, she went
to the park every day so she
could spy on the blue ones . . .

admire the yellow ones
with the purple dots . . .

and chase after all the pink ones.

When it was time to go, she always asked, "Can I bring one home?"

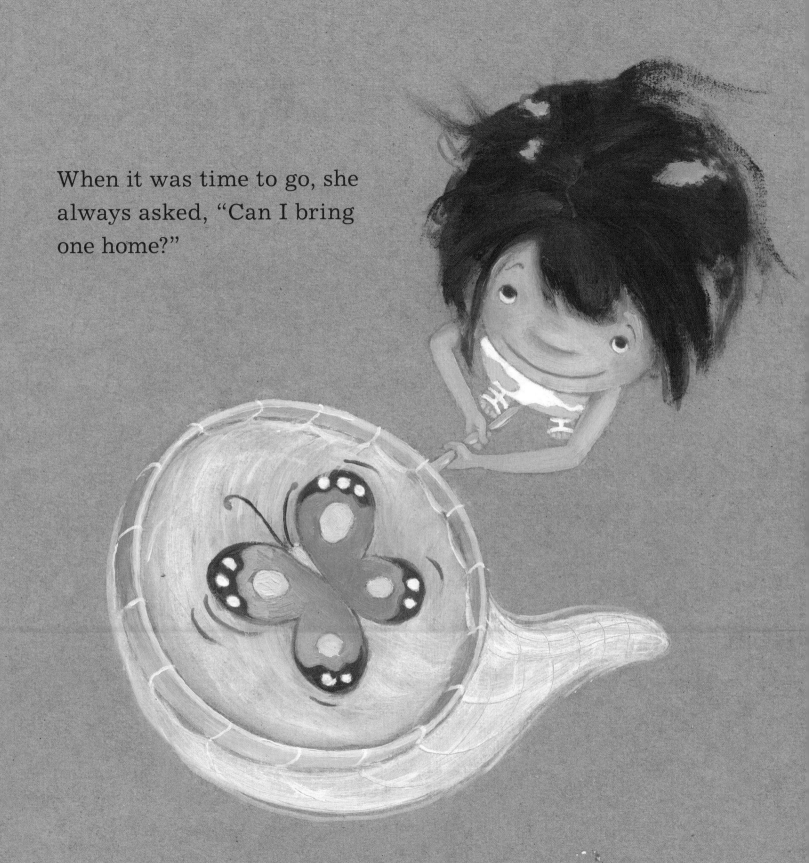

And her mom would reply, "No, it wouldn't be right."

One day, her dad bought her a painters' box.
He said, "Paint the butterflies and bring them home."

So she did.

As it turned out, she was quite good.

And she brought the butterflies home.

But when the summer ended, as summers do,
the butterflies bid farewell.

Once again Claudia asked to bring one home.
"No, it wouldn't be right," said her mom.
"Don't stop painting," added her dad.

But Claudia didn't feel like painting anymore,
and she stashed her paint box out of sight.

And once winter arrived,
there was truly nothing left to paint.

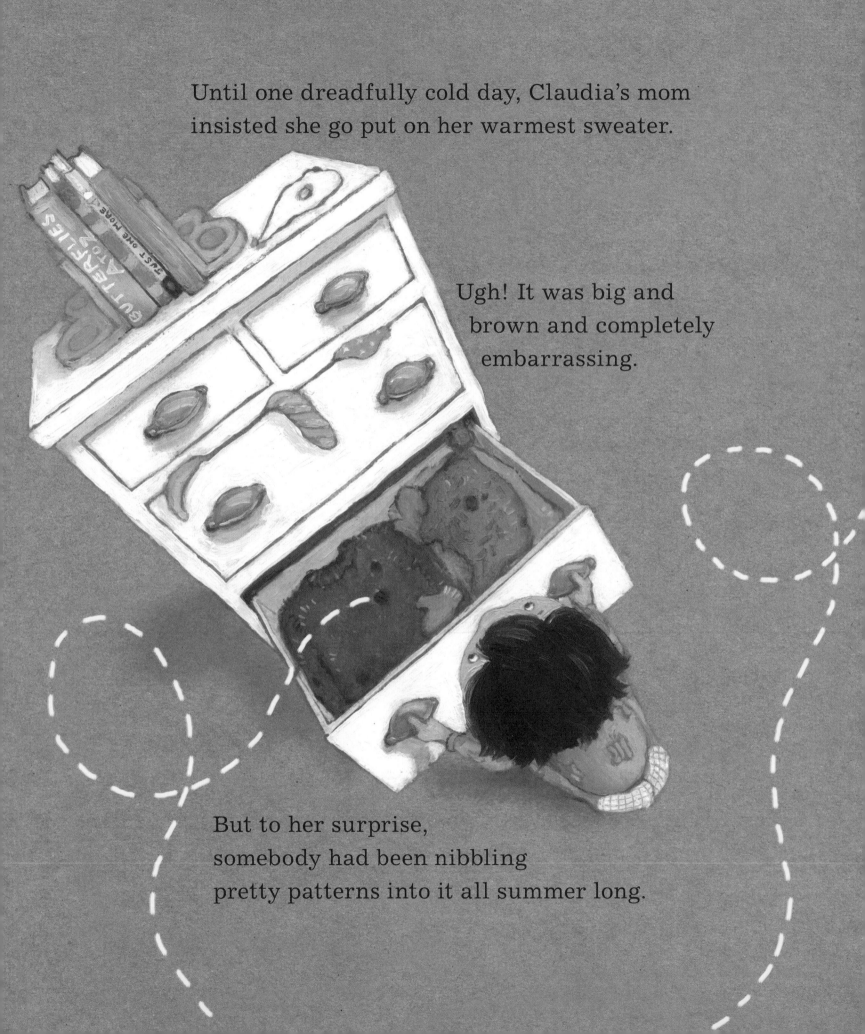

Until one dreadfully cold day, Claudia's mom insisted she go put on her warmest sweater.

Ugh! It was big and brown and completely embarrassing.

But to her surprise, somebody had been nibbling pretty patterns into it all summer long.

And when she spied the little moth, she felt a flutter of excitement.

It might not be right,
thought Claudia . . .

. . . but Moth made
the perfect butterfly.

Until he discovered
the window!

YiiiKeS!

PiNG! PaNG!

WhoOOa!

OooPs!

And the day went along something like that.

Then the sun set, and
quite miraculously,

Moth sat quiet.

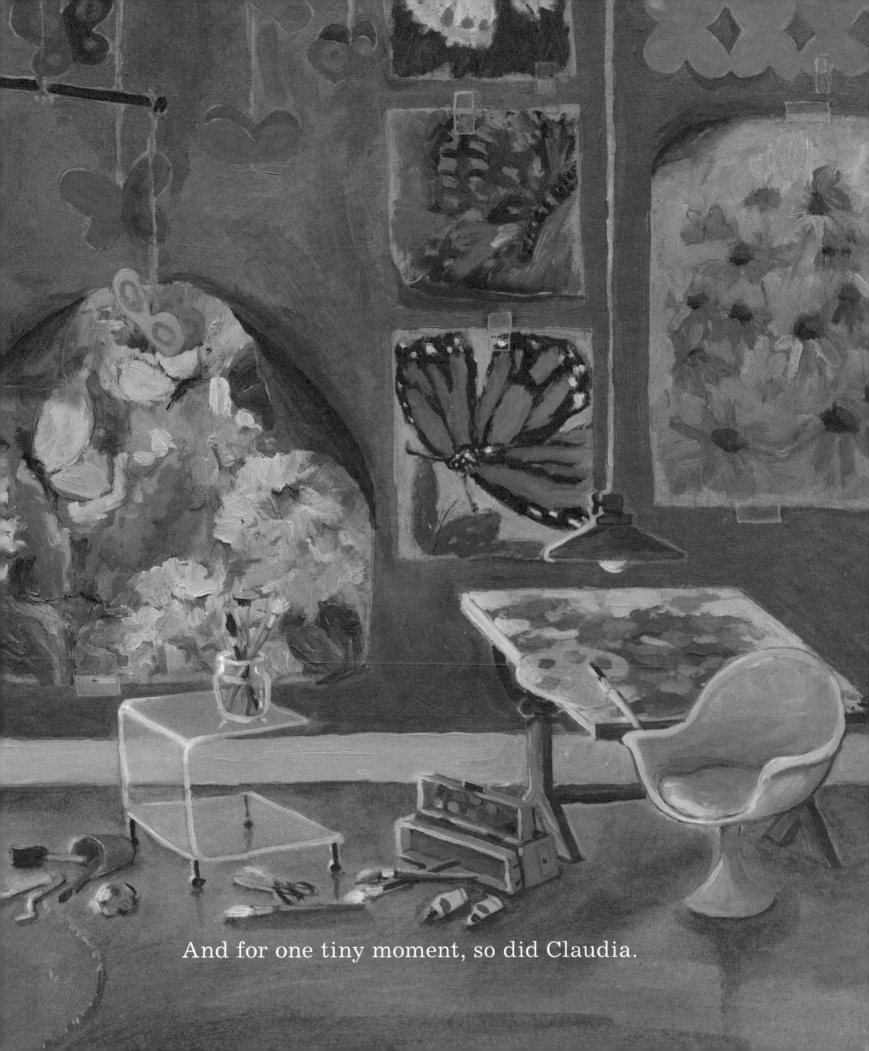

And for one tiny moment, so did Claudia.

"It's only snowflakes," said Claudia. She opened the window to show him . . .

Claudia burst out of the
apartment and ran down
to the street!

The city was never so quiet,
and the snow was never
so endless.

She blinked
and blinked,
but it was impossible
to tell Moth
from a snowflake.
The pretty patterns
melted too quickly
into her mittens
until . . .

PIop!

Only Moth wasn't quite
a butterfly anymore.

Claudia rushed him back inside and laid him under her light to dry.

Then something magnificent happened.

He flittered, he fluttered, he shined, and he shimmered.

Just like the snowflakes.

It was time for
Claudia to paint Moth.

So she could always remember him.

For Anthony, who always reminds me
that I wake up in the spring.

VIKING
An imprint of Penguin Random House LLC
375 Hudson Street
New York, New York 10014

First published in the United States of America by Viking,
an imprint of Penguin Random House LLC, 2017

Copyright © 2017 by Jennifer Hansen Rolli

LIBRARY OF CONGRESS CATALOGING-IN-PUBLICATION DATA IS AVAILABLE
ISBN: 9780425288337

Manufactured in China
Book design by Nancy Brennan   Set in Excelsior

The illustrations in this book are painted
with oils on brown paper.

1   3   5   7   9   10   8   6   4   2